Ziba Came on a Boat

Written by Liz Lofthouse
Illustrated by Robert Ingpen

PENGUIN|VIKING

Ziba came on a boat. A soggy old fishing boat
that creaked and moaned as it rose and fell,
rose and fell, across an endless sea...

Thoughts of home washed over Ziba like the surge of the sea washing over the deck.

She heard the laughter of children and the gentle sound of sheep grazing on the hillside.

She felt the cool mountain air on her cheeks as
she ran with her cousins down the rocky slope
to collect water from the mountain stream.

They laughed as they splashed each other with
icy water, and carried the heavy clay pots
to the warmth of the mud-brick house.

Ziba smelled the rich spices of
the evening meal.

She helped her aunties prepare
the flatbread cooked in the tandur,
and tasted the cool, smooth texture
of the goat's milk yoghurt her
mother made.

She saw her mother sitting at the wooden
loom, weaving coloured wool to make a rug.

Up and down went the wool, in and out,
like the boat weaving through the murky sea.

As the boat drifted through the night,
Ziba's thoughts drifted, too.

In her mind, she sat with her father,
playing with the doll he had given her.

He told her stories and poems of long ago.
She felt the strength of his arms and
she gazed into his peaceful face.

A cool wind blew across the swirling sea.

Ziba remembered the cold winter nights
at home.

Winter had lasted so much longer that year, and the shadow cast by the mountains to the east seemed to creep closer than ever before. The darkness spread, seeping into the quiet corners of the peaceful village.

No longer able to attend school, Ziba hid from the world behind the thick earthen walls of her home.

The sea roared and thrashed
at the boat like an angry beast.
The waves became fierce, and Ziba's
thoughts grew fearful and sad.

Gunfire echoed through the village. Angry voices
surrounded her. Clutching her mother's hand,
Ziba ran on and on through the night, far away
from the madness until there was
only darkness and quiet.

Ziba shivered, and huddled closer to her mother
in the crowded hull. Her mother's eyes were full
of hope and her lullaby sweet as honey.

Ziba drifted into sleep.

Her dream was warm and cosy.
Smiling faces welcomed her to
a new land. Here she could live
without fear. Here she would
be free to learn and laugh,
and dance again.

'*Azadi*,' her mother whispered. 'Freedom.'

And the boat rose and fell, rose and fell,
across an endless sea . . .

For my beautiful daughters Lucy and Sophie, and for our Afghan friends, who have given us an insight
into a different life, and who inspire us with their courage and determination – Liz Lofthouse

VIKING

Published by the Penguin Group
Penguin Group (Australia)
250 Camberwell Road
Camberwell, Victoria 3124, Australia
(a division of Pearson Australia Group Pty Ltd)
Penguin Group (USA) Inc.
375 Hudson Street, New York, New York 10014, USA
Penguin Group (Canada)
90 Eglinton Avenue East, Suite 700,
Toronto ON M4P 2Y3, Canada
(a division of Pearson Penguin Canada Inc.)
Penguin Books Ltd
80 Strand, London WC2R 0RL, England
Penguin Ireland
25 St Stephen's Green, Dublin 2, Ireland
(a division of Penguin Books Ltd)
Penguin Books India Pvt Ltd
11, Community Centre, Panchsheel Park, New Delhi -110 017, India
Penguin Group (NZ)
67 Apollo Drive, Rosedale, North Shore 0632, New Zealand
(a division of Pearson New Zealand Ltd)
Penguin Books (South Africa) (Pty) Ltd
24 Sturdee Avenue, Rosebank, Johannesburg 2196, South Africa

Penguin Books Ltd, Registered Offices: 80 Strand, London WC2R 0RL, England

First published by Penguin Group (Australia), 2007

3 5 7 9 10 8 6 4 2

Text copyright © Liz Lofthouse, 2007
Illustrations copyright © Robert Ingpen, 2007

Text and cover design by John Canty © Penguin Group (Australia)
Author photograph (Liz) by Tim Lofthouse
Typeset in 26/34 Centaur
Colour separation by Splitting Image Colour Studio
Printed and bound by Imago Productions, Singapore

National Library of Australia
Cataloguing-in-Publication data:
Lofthouse, Liz.
Ziba came on a boat.

ISBN : 978 0 670 02861 0.

1.Immigrant children - Juvenile fiction. I. Ingpen,
Robert, 1936- . II. Title.

A823.4

puffin.com.au